Hannah and the Ramadan Gift

By **Qasim Rashid**
Illustrated by **Aaliya Jaleel**

VIKING

When her dada jaan gently shook her awake,
Hannah Noor opened her eyes slowly, confused by the
darkness. The sun hadn't even risen yet. But when she saw
her grandfather smiling down at her, she remembered.

"Ramadan Mubarak!" shouted Hannah, jumping out of bed.

Hannah had been counting down to the first day of Ramadan, the holy month of fasting for Muslims, and now it was finally here.

"Can I fast this year?" Hannah asked. Going from dawn to sunset without eating for a whole month seemed hard to Hannah, but now that she was eight, she was surely old enough. How proud her grandma, Dadi Jaan, would have been of her today.

"Not yet, my dear," Dada Jaan said. "Fasting is for grown-ups, not for growing children."

"But if I can't fast, then how can I celebrate Ramadan?"

"By saving the world," replied Dada Jaan with a smile. "Hurry up now, let's join the others for sehri before the sun comes up."

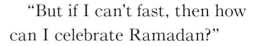

When Hannah heard Dada Jaan's
response and smelled the food of sehri, the
special breakfast of Ramadan, she forgot
her disappointment.

After sehri and the morning
prayer, it was time to get ready
for school.

"Let's stop at the soup kitchen on the way to school,"
Dada Jaan said.

"Why?" Hannah asked. "Don't we have plenty of soup
at home?"

Dada Jaan explained, "The soup isn't for us.
When we fast during Ramadan, we feel hungry,
and it reminds us that, all over the world,
there are people who don't have enough
food—so we must help them."

"But the world has so many people—how can we help them all?" Hannah asked.

"We can help our neighbors," Dada Jaan replied, "and that's worth the world."

Later that day at school, Hannah played with her friend Maria.
"That's the bell. We should go back to class," said Hannah.
"Wait!" cried Maria. "I lost my grandma's necklace!"
"What does it look like?"
"It's gold with a green gemstone. Can you help me find it?"
"Let's look in all the places we played today," Hannah said.
But the necklace wasn't on the basketball court or the kickball field.

"I know! Let's look in the jungle gym," said
Hannah finally. And there it was!
"It must've fallen off when I did that backflip.
Thank you, Hannah!"

Hannah rushed into class after the bell stopped ringing.

"Next time, please make sure you are on time," said Mrs. Holmes sternly.

"But I was just—" Hannah wanted to explain, but her teacher had already started reading again. Ramadan had just begun and already Hannah had gotten in trouble. Helping neighbors wasn't as easy as Dada Jaan made it seem.

On the eleventh day, Dada Jaan woke Hannah early before sunrise. "Shall we save the world again today, Dada Jaan?" Hannah asked excitedly.

Then she remembered that today was also an important day at school—the big science fair—and she did not want to be late.

"Don't worry," Dada Jaan said. "We're up in plenty of time to stop at the shelter before you go to school. Come, let's go."

"But, Dada Jaan, the people at the shelter won't
know that we're the ones who donated the clothes."
"Why does that matter, Hannah?" asked Dada
Jaan. "Sometimes it's enough to help people simply
out of love. Besides," he whispered with a wink, "all
the best superheroes work in secret, don't they?"

When Hannah got to school, she got ready
for the science fair.

"Amazing model, Hannah!" her friend Dani
said as Hannah arranged her model replica of
Abbas ibn Firnas's flying machine.

"Thanks!" said Hannah. "What's yours?"
"It's a globe showing the dates and flight
path for Amelia Earhart, the first woman to fly
solo around the world. Ooh, look, Maria made
a robot!" Dani set his model down and ran off.

"Dani, wait!" The globe was rolling off the table. Hannah lunged and caught it just before it smashed into the ground.

That was close! Hannah thought. She put the globe back on the table before anyone noticed.

"Dani wins!"

Hannah was happy for Dani. He was a good friend and the globe was amazing. But no one knew that Hannah had saved the day.

"How was the science fair, Hannah?" asked Dada Jaan when he picked her up.

"Fine," said Hannah quietly. Why didn't she feel happy about doing the right thing? Dada Jaan made it seem so easy.

On Saturday, twenty days of Ramadan had passed. "Remember, you have a playdate with Sarah," called Hannah's mother. Sarah's family had just moved into their neighborhood.

"But I was going to work on my art project today," objected Hannah. "And I don't even know Sarah."

"Hannah, that's not very nice. We need to welcome new neighbors like family."

"I'll make you a deal, Hannah," Dada Jaan said. "I'll go with you, and if you're not having fun, we can leave whenever you want, okay?"

"I won't have fun!" muttered Hannah, but she went with Dada Jaan anyway.

They ate delicious kanafeh
that Sarah's mom had made.

They looked at pictures of Sarah's
friends from her old school.

Pretty soon they had lost track of time altogether.
"Ready to go?" asked Dada Jaan.
"But we haven't finished our game!" said Hannah and
Sarah at the same time.

When they got home, Dada Jaan showed Hannah an old family photo album.

Hannah couldn't believe what she saw.

"This is from the year we moved to this place. We didn't know anyone. We didn't speak the language."

"So what did you do?" asked Hannah.

"It was the kindness of our friends that got us through," said Dada Jaan. "And," he said, twinkling at Hannah, "it probably helped that your dadi jaan was happy to feed our neighbors the best butter chicken in the world!"

That evening when Hannah thought about her Ramadan, she was sad. First she got in trouble after helping Maria. Then she did the right thing to help Dani, but she felt sad that no one knew. And she was ashamed about how she did not want to play with Sarah at first.

It was the last day of Ramadan.
"Sunset during Ramadan is called . . ."
"Iftar!" said Hannah.

"That's right," said Dada Jaan. "At iftar, we break our fast.
And when the sun sets on the last day of Ramadan . . ."
"It's the Eid al-Fitr celebration!" Hannah exclaimed.

Dada Jaan smiled. "Do you think you made the world a better place by helping your neighbors this Ramadan?"

"I tried," Hannah responded. "But I don't think it worked."

"I wouldn't be too sure about that," said Dada Jaan.

The sun was shining the next day. It was finally Eid! Hannah and her family headed to the mosque for Eid prayer. The mosque, like their home, was decorated with Ramadan lights, and the air was filled with the wonderful aroma of her favorite Eid desserts.

After Eid prayer, they visited the cemetery to remember Dadi Jaan and other loved ones.

They got home for the Eid party just as their guests started pouring in, exclaiming,

"EID MUBARAK!"

Hannah's whole world was there to celebrate Eid! Her cousins from out of town, her friends who attended the church across the street. The neighbors who attended a synagogue right by their mosque. The Sikh family who ran the soup kitchen at the local gurdwara.

Everyone was hugging her and saying, "Eid Mubarak, Hannah!"

They ate delicious kheer, gulab jamuns, and jalebis. They hugged and laughed.

"Race you to the last gulab jamun!" said Dada Jaan.

But Hannah had something else on her mind. "How do I really know if I've helped the world this Ramadan, Dada Jaan?"

"Well, let's see. Did you help your friends when they needed you?"

Hannah thought about Maria. "Yes."

"Did you help others simply out of love?"

Hannah nodded as she thought about Dani's globe.

"And did you show love to those who had no one else?"
"I think so," said Hannah as she thought about Sarah.
"Then you have your answer," said Dada Jaan.

It would still be many
years before Hannah could
fast for Ramadan. But she'd
helped her neighbors—her
world—and that made this
the best Eid ever.

Author's Note

My earliest memories of Ramadan are from the late 1980s in Pakistan, and then the early 1990s in Chicago. Ramadan is based on the lunar calendar, so it comes ten days earlier every year. I recall the excitement of the first fast, the wonderful aromas that filled the home every evening, and the countdown until the last fast. I recall the joy in going door-to-door to give our neighbors gifts, of giving charity to the less fortunate. The words of my parents repeating over and over again, "Prophet Muhammad (peace be upon him) taught that our mission, our purpose, is to serve all humanity. That's what Ramadan is all about." I recall the elation of getting Eidi (money from elders) on Eid, only to spend it on candy and games at the store the next day. But most of all, I remember the comfort and innocence of a time when life was simpler. When we reflected on what we've been blessed with, strengthened ties of kinship, and did our best to save humanity, serving one person at a time.

For my children,
Hassan, Hashim, and Hannah Noor,
who inspired this book. —Q.R.

For my family and friends,
who fill Ramadan with warmth and love. —A.J.

VIKING
An imprint of Penguin Random House LLC, New York

First published in the United States of America by Viking,
an imprint of Penguin Random House LLC, 2021

Text copyright © 2021 by Qasim Rashid
Illustrations copyright © 2021 by Aaliya Jaleel

LIBRARY OF CONGRESS CATALOGING-IN-PUBLICATION DATA IS AVAILABLE.
Manufactured in China

ISBN 9780593114667
1 3 5 7 9 10 8 6 4 2

Design by Lucia Baez and Jim Hoover • Text set in Binny Old Style

Illustrations were digitally drawn in Procreate.